The
GLENELG
COUNTRY
SCHOOL

A
BIRTHDAY
·BOOK·

Presented in honor of

Ryan Lundergan
on his fourth birthday

·Given by·

Mom & Dad
November 9, 2001

A Note to Parents

Eyewitness Readers is a compelling new program
for beginning readers, designed in conjunction with
leading literacy experts, including Dr. Linda Gambrell,
President of the National Reading Conference and past
board member of the International Reading Association.

Eyewitness has become the most trusted name in
illustrated books, and this new series combines the highly
visual *Eyewitness* approach with engaging, easy-to-read
stories. Each *Eyewitness Reader* is guaranteed to capture
a child's interest while developing his or her reading
skills, general knowledge, and love of reading.

The four levels of *Eyewitness Readers* are aimed at
different reading abilities, enabling you to choose the
books that are exactly right for your children:

Level One – Beginning to read
Level Two – Beginning to read alone
Level Three – Reading alone
Level Four – Proficient readers

The "normal" age at which a child begins to read
can be anywhere from three to eight years old, so these
levels are intended only as a general guideline.

No matter which level you select, you can be sure
that you are helping your child learn to read, then
read to learn!

A DK PUBLISHING BOOK
www.dk.com
Editors Jennifer Siklós and Caroline Bingham
Designer Michelle Baxter
Senior Editor Linda Esposito
Deputy Managing Art Editor Jane Horne
US Editor Regina Kahney
Production Kate Oliver
Photography Richard Leeney

Reading Consultant
Linda B. Gambrell, Ph.D.

First American Edition, 1998
2 4 6 8 10 9 7 5 3
Published in the United States by
DK Publishing, Inc.
95 Madison Avenue, New York, New York 10016

Library of Congress Cataloging-in-Publication Data
Royston, Angela
   Truck trouble / written by Angela Royston.
     p. cm. -- (Eyewitness readers. Level 1)
   Summary: Describes a truck driver's rig and some of the problems
he encounters as he picks up and delivers his cargo.
ISBN 0-7894-2958-6
   1. Truck driving--Juvenile literature. [1. Truck driving. 2. Trucks.] I. Title. II. Series.
TL230.15.R67   1998
   629.28'44--dc21

97-44988
CIP
AC

Color reproduction by Colourscan, Singapore
Printed and bound in Belgium by Proost

The publisher would like to thank the following for their kind permission to reproduce their photographs:
Key: t=top, b=below, l=left, r=right, c=center
Pictor International: (14-15)
Jacket: **Pictor International:** front (background)
Additional photography by Andy Crawford (26bl & 32 - bolt), Ray Moller (30-31) and Alex Wilson (13t).

The publisher would also like to thank Rick Roberton at Western Truck Limited.
Special thanks to John Scholey at W Scholey & Son for the use of his truck, time and premises.

DK EYEWITNESS READERS

BEGINNING 1 TO READ

Truck Trouble

BE-16-88

Written by Angela Royston

DK PUBLISHING, INC.

John got up very early
to make a special delivery.
He climbed up two steps
into his big blue truck.

John looked at the map.
Today was no day to get lost!
Then he started the truck,
checked the mirrors, and set off.

mirror

At a service station,
John checked the engine.
It needed some oil.
Then he filled up the fuel tank.

fuel tank

He looked at
the shiny engine.
"Don't let me down!"
he said.
"I can't be late!"

Next he had to pick up the cargo.
A forklift raised big boxes
into the back of John's truck.

There were also some small boxes
marked "Special Delivery."
John put these in the truck too.

John was in a hurry,
but he was also
very hungry.

He pulled into a truck stop
for breakfast.

John's friend Paul arrived
in his milk tanker.
He joined John for breakfast.

But John couldn't stop for long.
He had deliveries to make!

John drove on to the freeway.
It was jammed with traffic.
Cars and trucks beeped their horn

ohn had to deliver the big boxes
o a nearby factory.
He left the freeway at the next exit.

John waved to the workers as he drove into the factory.

The workers helped him
unload the big boxes.

"I'm in a hurry,"
John told them.
"I've got another delivery
to make."
Soon he was on his way.
But there was trouble ahead.

A van had broken down!
John slammed on his brakes.
His truck screeched to a halt.

The road was very narrow.
John's truck was too wide
to get past the van.

John used his radio to call for help.
He also warned all other drivers
to stay away from that road.

Soon John saw flashing lights.
It was a tow truck!
The tow truck
towed the van
to a garage.

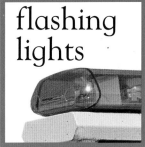

flashing
lights

When the road was clear
John hurried on his way.
But there was more trouble ahead!

Boom! Boom!

John drove into a thunderstorm.

Rain began to pour down.

John turned on
the windshield wipers.

wiper

He drove very slowly.

"This isn't my day!"
he groaned.

John drove on and on.
Finally the rain stopped.
He pulled over to eat his lunch.

Then he rested
on a bunk
in the back of the cab.
He fell fast asleep!

cab

When he woke up, John thought,
"Now I'm in trouble!"

BANG!
"Oh no! A flat tire!"
John grabbed
his tools and
the spare wheel.

wheel

He unscrewed
the bolts and
took off the wheel.

bolt

Then he put on the spare.
It was hard work!

John drove into town.
He had to wait for
the traffic light
to turn green.

traffic
light

"Hurry up!" thought John.
He was almost late
for his special delivery.

At last John arrived.
There was no time to spare!
He unloaded the boxes marked
"Special Delivery."

John was just in time for the party at the new children's hospital.

Inside the special boxes
were piles of toys.
"Thank you!" shouted the children.
"It was no trouble!" said John.

Picture Word List

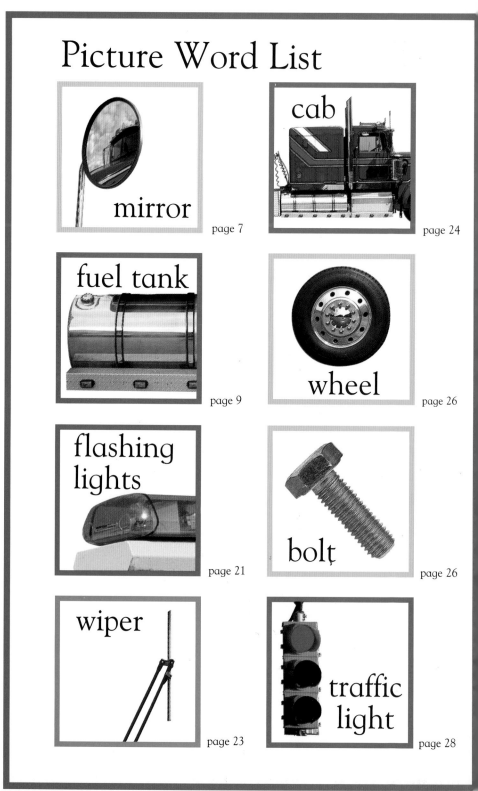

mirror
page 7

cab
page 24

fuel tank
page 9

wheel
page 26

flashing lights
page 21

bolt
page 26

wiper
page 23

traffic light
page 28

▣ EYEWITNESS READERS

Level 1 *Beginning to Read*

A Day at Greenhill Farm
Truck Trouble
Tale of a Tadpole
Surprise Puppy!
Duckling Days
A Day at Seagull Beach
Whatever the Weather
Busy, Buzzy Bee

Level 2 *Beginning to Read Alone*

Dinosaur Dinners
Fire Fighter!
Bugs! Bugs! Bugs!
Slinky, Scaly Snakes!
Animal Hospital
The Little Ballerina
Munching, Crunching, Sniffing, and Snooping
The Secret Life of Trees

Level 3 *Reading Alone*

Spacebusters
Beastly Tales
Shark Attack!
Titanic
Invaders from Outer Space
Movie Magic
Plants Bite Back!
Time Traveler

Level 4 *Proficient Readers*

Days of the Knights
Volcanoes
Secrets of the Mummies
Pirates!
Horse Heroes
Trojan Horse
Micromonsters
Going for Gold!

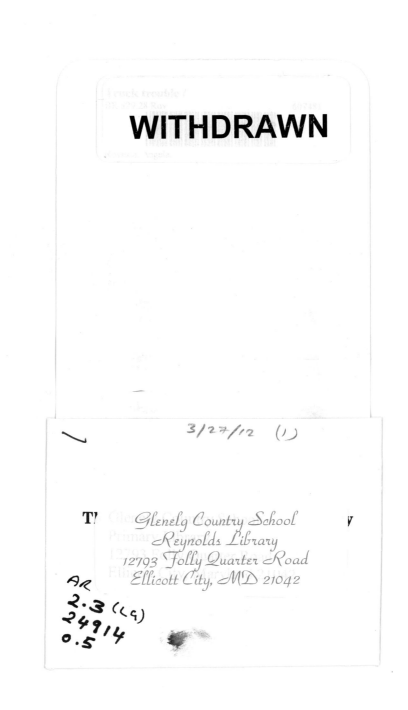

3/27/12 (1)